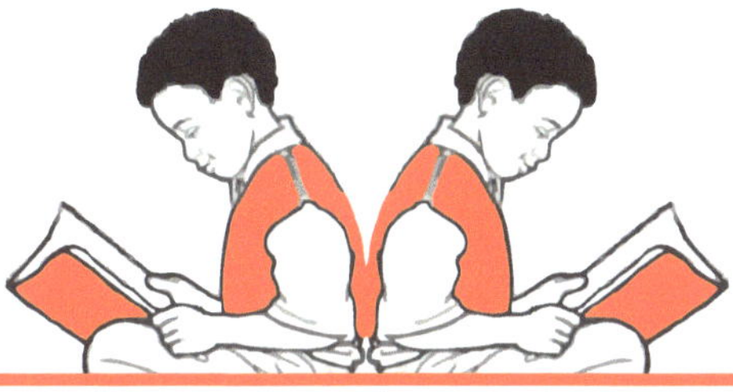

THIS BOOK BELONGS TO

Icon Publishing Limited
P. O. Box OD 972
Odorkor, Accra
Ghana
www.facebook.com/myicongh
www.twitter.com/myicongh
+233 (0)23 3505 055,

iconpublishingltd@gmail.com
iconpublishing@ymail.com
enquiries.icongh@gmail.com

Books published by Icon Publishing Limited are available at special discounts for bulk purchases in Ghana by corporations, institutions, and other organisations. For more information, please call the Special Markets Department on +233 (0)23 3505 055 or send an e-mail to iconpublishingltd@gmail.com.

Cover and Interior Design by iCON-gh +233 24 4890 432

ISBN: 978-9988-8567-2-4

THE FATE OF THE DECEITFUL TORTOISE

AND ANOTHER TALE FROM AFRICA*

*THE SILLY BLIND MAN (A FOLKTALE WITH AN ADULT THEME)

Dan Odei

Kwame Insaidoo

This Nigerian folktale shows what happens when the deceitful tortoise plays a vicious game on animals trading at the Nkwoagu market.

Nkwoagu was the biggest market area in all the land, so all the animals from the neighbouring villages, hamlets, and towns went there to sell and market their wares every day. When the clever tortoise saw them marketing their food, and all kinds of jewellery and diamonds, he decided to concoct a diabolical plan to steal their items.

One cloudy day, he hid in a small pit, adjacent to the market, and when the market was crowded with many animals buying, selling, and haggling over these wares, he shouted loud and clear:

All animals in this market, listen to what is coming to get you,

Because you have disobediently violated the traditional beliefs of the sacred market of Nkwoagu by selling, haggling, and buying in a sacred place,

This sacred place is not meant for such abuse,

So calamity from the gods will befall whomever the gods catch right now.

The gods are on their way to catch you all right now—you better run.

When the animals in the market heard him sing the song twice, they fled and left their wares behind. They knew that the market place had originally been a place of sacrifice for the gods, but the stubborn chiefs had converted the site to a market place, much to the gods' annoyance. As quickly as the animals ran out of the market, the tortoise came out of his hiding place and stole the most expensive and valuable wares he could find.

The next day, when the animals returned to the market to have a look around, some of the merchants discovered that most of their valuable wares like diamond necklaces and gold ornaments had been stolen. About a month later, the animals decided to return to Nkwoagu market to sell their wares, believing that the traditional gods would have mercy on them, knowing that they had to buy and sell to survive. As before, when the selling, buying, and haggling of the merchants and buyers were at their peak, the tortoise hid in the same pit adjacent to the market and sang loudly again.

This time his song created the same amount of chaos and pandemonium, with the animals running for dear life trampling over each other to get away from

On hearing the tortoise sing, the animals fled and left their wares behind the market, so once again, the tortoise achieved what he set out to do. By sowing confusion among the animals, he was able to steal their valuable wares.

The next day the animals were incensed about what was happening because they could see that somebody was playing a clever trick on them, so they hired the owl to find out who was really singing.

The owl disguised himself by painting half of his face with charcoal and the other half with chalk, and then he hid behind the same small pit adjacent to the market. As usual the animals gathered in the market to sell their wares, but no sooner had they gathered than the deceitful tortoise began to blow his large horn and sing his song, insulting the animals and accusing them of being ungrateful to the traditional gods. They had better run for their dear lives, he warned, because the gods were going to catch them red-handed for violating their sacred site. As usual the animals ran away, but the owl eased his way behind the tortoise and saw him stealing the valuable goods of the merchants from the market.

The owl shouted in excitement and called all the animals together to come and see the "traditional gods" who were stealing their wares. When the animals gathered around the tortoise, they wanted to kill him right then and there for deceiving them and stealing their wares, but they decided to collectively impose a death sentence on him. They locked him up in a tiny hut to await execution by the lion the following day.

The tortoise was awaiting execution, deathly afraid as the minutes ticked away and daybreak slowly gnawed the night away. At dawn the tortoise's wife was allowed to visit him in his small hut. When she got inside, the tortoise asked his wife to run home to bring his ogiri (a blackish condiment made from fermented melon seeds) and rub it all over his body. The wife ran as fast as she could, brought the ogiri, and rubbed it all over his body. Then she quietly left the hut.

The next morning all the animals assembled for the execution; some were impatient for the tortoise to be executed for playing deadly games on them, but when the animals approached him, the smell of the ogiri on his body was so awful that it was unbearable. The centipede said, "The poor bastard is already dead, so throw him away. Can't you all smell the scent of a dead tortoise?"

The tortoise's wife rubbing the ogiri all over his body

All the animals echoed, "Yes the poor bastard is dead, so throw him away." They were glad to see the deceitful tortoise dead, so they threw him into a pit and left to market the wares at their market in Nkwoagu. When the tortoise saw that all the animals were gone, he slowly moved away from the pit and went home to thank his lovely wife.

The animals throwing the tortoise into a pit

The moral here relates to the fact that traditional people abhorred cheats, liars, and people who employed deceptive methods to get ahead in society. The sense of moral justice that prevailed here was that the perpetrator was caught red-handed and the society could impose its sentence on him. The elders did not want to punish innocent people who were merely accused without knowing for sure that they had committed an offense, so they went to great lengths to insure that a criminal was caught red-handed in the commission of an act.

Finally, sentences had to be harsh enough to serve as deterrent to others, to insure the maintenance of stable societies, where law and order prevailed.

Answer the following questions:

1. a) What did all the animals from the neighbouring villages, hamlets, and towns go to do at Nkwoagu?

   b) What went through the tortoise's mind when he saw them?

2. Describe all the tricks the tortoise played on the other animals?

3. a) How did the Owl catch the tortoise stealing the valuable goods of the merchants?

   b) What sentence was imposed on the tortoise?

4. How did the tortoise escape the sentence?

5. What have you learned from this folktale?

6. Find the meaning of the following words in the dictionary;

   i. Wares

   ii. Concoct

   iii. Diabolical

   iv. Haggling

   v. Violated

   vi. Chaos

   vii. Pandemonium

viii. Incensed

ix. Gnawed

x. Disguised

7. Give three adjectives that can be used to describe the tortoise in this story.

8. Which one word can be used for the following items: diamond necklaces, gold ornaments, bangle?

The Silly Blind Man

A Gambian folktale about the shenanigans of the silly blind man.

Long and long ago, there lived a blind man in the village of Santoba. All day long he spent his time in married women's homes, looking to make love to them when their husbands were at work.

One day he went to the market square and heard the men talking about the most beautiful woman in the village who had just gotten married to the wealthiest man in the village. This treacherous blind man was determined to go to the house of this newly wedded woman with the wicked intent of attempting to trick her into making love to him. He began to contrive the diabolical means of getting into her house, showering expensive gifts on the lady, lying to her that her husband had many other mistresses and therefore could not really love her alone, and finally convincing her to make love to him.

The day before he was to carry out his dastardly act, he informed his best friend of how he would easily trick the beautiful, newly wedded lady in the town to go to bed with him. Unfortunately for him, his best friend would have none of the blind man's treacherous behaviour of running after married women in Santoba, so he told the lady's husband of the silly blind man's wicked intentions.

The next day, early in the morning, the husband sent the wife alone to the farm, telling her that he was not feeling well and might join her later during the day, when the sun came up and he felt a little better. The husband was left alone in the house waiting impatiently for the silly blind man to come and meet him. He waited and waited for the silly blind man, and just as he was about to give up waiting for him, there was a knock at his door. And lo and behold, the silly blind man was standing at his door. The husband pretended to be a woman by changing his voice and asked the blind man to enter his room, which he did, thinking that he was speaking to the wife.

The husband, speaking like a woman, said to the blind man, "Hello, young man what brings you here?

The husband speaking like a woman to the blind man

What can I do for you? Did you come to see my husband? He has already gone to his farm, and I will join him in a few minutes."

The blind man, still believing that he had gotten the wife alone, began by telling her a lie, "You know, when I first saw you at the wedding ceremony, I thought you were a nice and intelligent woman, but I was surprised that you chose such a dim-witted man for a husband. You know the only thing he has going for him is his money. Do you know he is also a womanizer who has many mistresses? What makes you think he really loves you at all? You should know he doesn't.

The blind man continued, "I may be blind, but I am very rich and will take good care of you by making sure you do not have to go to farms to do the hard labour of weeding and confronting all those ugly and venomous snakes. I will take good care of you by letting you stay home and not having you do any hard or menial work. As you know, the menial work on the farm will destroy your beauty and make you age quickly."

He concluded, "Now, lady, tell me how much money you need right now for yourself."

The husband, pretending to be his wife, said, "I could use one hundred cowries." (Cowries were used as the local currency in those days.) The blind man pulled out one hundred cowries and gave them to him, still believing that he was speaking to the wife. The husband told the blind man that since he had so much money, he should double his gift and make it two hundred cowries. The blind man produced the two hundred cowries and gave it to the husband, adding, "You see, I am here for you. Anything you need, I can give it to you anytime and anyplace you need it."

The husband, still pretending to be the wife, said, "Since you are such a good man, why don't you give me your shirt and trousers now." The blind man removed his shirts and trousers and gave them to the husband. The blind man asked the husband, "What else can I do for you? You know I am all yours; so just name anything, and I will do it for you."

The husband said, "Why don't you give me your wallet, and then take off your underwear and stand here naked." The silly blind man gave his wallet to the husband, and then he removed all his clothes until he was naked and stood there stupidly before the husband.

The husband took all the blind man's clothes away, cleared his throat, and then said in his own real voice, "Hey, young man, you cannot see anything, but my wife has gone to the farm." The blind man felt ashamed at his silly behaviour and asked the husband for forgiveness. The husband called the chief and the elders of the village of Santoba to advise the blind man regarding his unsavoury behaviour.

The chief and his elders warned the blind man never to go after any man's wife because it could lead to his death or him being disgraced in the presence of the villagers. They advised him that it was improper and morally depraved behaviour to go after other men's wives or girlfriends and that he should learn to respect other people's relationships.

The elders told the blind man that going after other people's wives demonstrated that he did not have self-respect or discipline. If he had those attributes he would not have gone so far astray as to display such foolhardy behaviour as he had by taking off his clothes in front of a man pretending to be a woman.

The husband took all the blind man's clothes away

The chief concluded that not only was he physically blind, but he was also morally blind as demonstrated by his behaviour in the village, and he should go and change from his wicked ways.

The chief and elders also made it a point to advise the women of the village to be careful of lying men who came to them promising to give them the world in order to lure them to leave their husbands. The chief said, "If a naked man promises to give you clothes, look at him to see what he is wearing before allowing him to speak further to you. How can a naked man give you clothes when he does not even have any for himself?"

Answer the following questions:

1. What was the name of the village in which the blind man lived?

2. How did the blind man spend most of his time?

3. What did the blind man decide to do when he heard that the most beautiful woman in the village had married the wealthiest man in the village?

4. What were some of the tactics the blind man used in order to win the love of the most beautiful women in the village?

5. How did the beautiful woman's husband get to know of the blind man's intentions?

6. What did the husband do when he got to know of the blind man's evil intentions?

7. What did the chief and his elders say would happen to the blind man if he continued in his evil ways?

8. List all the adjectives in the second paragraph of the story.

9. Give synonyms for the following words as they have been used in the story.

   a. beautiful — (paragraph 2)

   b. wealthiest — (paragraph 2)

   c. treacherous — (paragraph 2)

   d. trick — (paragraph 2)

   e. silly — (paragraph 3)

   f. surprised — (paragraph 6)

   g. intelligent — (paragraph 6)

10. Find out the meanings of the following words and use them in sentences of your own:

    a. determined

    b. contrive

    c. wealthy

    d. intentions

    e. pretend

    f. disgrace

11. Give one word that can be used to describe the husband of the beautiful woman.